George Appleton Stockwell, Louis D. Norton

Our Choir

George Appleton Stockwell, Louis D. Norton

Our Choir

ISBN/EAN: 9783337298104

Printed in Europe, USA, Canada, Australia, Japan

Cover: Foto ©Andreas Hilbeck / pixelio.de

More available books at **www.hansebooks.com**

Our Choir.

BY THE SEXTON:

Author of the Forthcoming and Voluminous Work Entitled "THE CONFLICT BETWEEN THE MAN IN THE WALL-PEW AND THE NORTH-WINDOW AS WITNESSED BY THE CON— QUEROR OF THE ONE AND THE (AT LAST) CONTROLLER OF THE OTHER."

<u>ASSISTED BY</u>

GEO. A. STOCKWELL.

WILLIAM J. DANIELSON:
PROVIDENCE.

CONTENTS.

ı

TO

YOUR CHOIR,

THE MOST HARMONIOUS AND MELODIOUS,

THIS BOOK

IS RESPECTFULLY INSCRIBED BY THE

AUTHOR.

Our Choir.

—

THE OVERTURE.

—

HE desire for musical en-
lightenment and enter-
tainment found expres-
sion at first in timorous,
plaintive, diminuendo
suggestion. But it grew
and became bolder;
its pleading gathered
strength and volume, mounted up note by note,
chord upon chord, until this longing for greater
vocal and instrumental harmony burst forth

like a fanfare of trumpets in a "grand crescendo" demand.

The time had come. It stood tip-toe on the threshold. The voice of a choir, the skillful blending of the tenor, the bass, the alto and the soprano, must sing responsive to our yearnings. Longer delay would leave us stranded and forsaken upon a neglected shore with only the singing-sands to guide and to accompany, and as some of these sands were out of tune and past repair, there was sufficient cause for an uprising.

No longer could we sit by the way trying to bring our discordant harps into harmony, and look with equal minds upon the old and the young, who by tens and by twenties were passing on their way to more inviting fields where was "concord of sweet sounds," without bestowing upon us so much as a nod of recognition, and apparently unmindful of our existence, or did they know, painful thought, that our pipes were cracked and wheezy, that our cymbals had yielded up to time's wrack, and that our strings and bows had lost their cunning.

Even some of our own members, the young and sprightly, were often afar — not in their accustomed places. Where were they? Was it not possible that "smart choirs" elsewhere were attractive, and was there not a suspicion that our humdrum-drooning in congregational-singing was repellant? Other churches were adding power to strength, and reaching out and laying hands upon the people, while ours was where it had been since its time was—stock still, and, also, apparently, withdrawing into itself and closing the door behind it.

The young and up-members were few in number, aye, and grew less, and the few was a harrassed-few, for they were tongue-lashed, and held up in scorn for running to other churches, seeking after false gods, and frivolities in general; and these young folks, bold beyond belief, had the audacity to reply: "Why, we want something new, something interesting, something lively."

Had it come to this? Our members in good and regular standing confessing to a debasing longing for novelties, and, worse than all, for something "lively." With reason might we despair of ever reaching Pisgah's heights when the flower of the flock went a-gadding. Our pillar-members were hewn out of Pilgrim stock, several generations removed. They were "set in their way," and, indeed, sat in the way as if held down by bolts and rivets.

Good Deacon Grampus was the chief pillar, aye, and sleeper, the chorister, and the chief singer ; and also, the chief block that stopped progress in the musical way. He declared, often with vehemence and gestures, that he hoped to be done with the cares of this life "before a choir riz up ter sing in that gal'ry " Indeed, he was the "chiefest" singer, and often a solo singer. When he faced the audience, pulled the stops of all his pipes, and his voice fell upon the innocent melody, then was there something to hear.

In his early singing-school days, Deacon Grampus had courted the intimate acquaintance of the "good old tunes,"—Old Hundred, Boylston, Dedham, Silver Street, Windham, Hamburg, Duke Street, and many more. He announced often — it was unnecessary — as if it were some·thing in his favor, something remarkable, since he sang so well, that he did not know one note from another. "But," said the deacon, "when I tackle one o' the good old tunes, I kin make it go." He could, and if he had kept on unobstructed in his musical, or vocal way, he would have made every member of the congregation go—go on the run with a finger in each ear as trespassers in the land of Og fled from the roar of the leader of the Bashan herd.

His voice had no soft, lullaby notes in it; 'twas'nt pitched that way; it was a wind instrument, cracked, hoarse, and powerful, like a foghorn with a rusty throat. In the social meetings, Deacon Grampus "started all the tunes." Whatever the hymn might be, it was adapted to one of the old melodies. It has been whispered around that some frivolous and worldly persons attended the meetings merely to hear Deacon

Grampus sing, and to see how neatly he could adapt a hymn in one metre to a tune intended for a hymn in another metre. Somewhere near the end of the line the voice, apparently surprised at the surplus of words or notes, that they did not fit, turned a somersault, made a hop, skip and a jump, and came out evenly and staccato on the last note and syllable.

II.

MAJOR(ITY) AND MINOR(ITY) AIRS.

—

Sister Snug.

THE call to arms had been sounded. It was it and nothing else,—the call to meeting to consider the question of maintaining a choir, and, according to the determined purpose of some members, a minority with few members, but many words, to give it such repulse—defeat, decisive and destructive, that it would never rise again to menace the peace, and to endanger the church.

"We'll show them," said an intellectual and obstructive member, with an impressive wave of his forefinger, — "we'll show the advocates of the sinful pleasures of the world, that they cannot set up their idols in this church."

But progress has a bold front, is up and doing when aroused, and is cunning and practical. While the no-choir party hung weights on arguments, or soared on "elocution's wings," the choir party went a-hunting for votes, bagged them, and at the proper time the result of ballot coursing would appear.

The choir party caught the majority before the meeting "to sit and to sift" was called, for, if the vote led by the pillars were against the project, then there would be no reconsideration for a year. Deacon Grampus would say, "What's did's did, an' can't be undid."

Therefore, the time had come to act — to act quickly. Not another year could the church remain on this sliding scale — sliding back — back into inactivity and the gloom of obscurity.

The meeting was interesting especially to the choir-party, with its bag of votes, and its majority tugging at the leash, when the long and " clinching arguments " against the choir were piled up in voluminous extravagance.

" I tell ye," said the deacon as he opened the meeting, " I'm agin any an' all choirs. I've ben here nigh onter fifty year, an' we've managed ter get erlong 'thout a choir. Ef we've got ter look ter a.choir fer ter build up Zion, we're in a dreffle bad way — past savin', an' not wuth savin'. "We don't want no choir, an' we ain't ergoin' ter hev no choir, nuther."

The deacon was right although he did not

mean what he said. The majority was determined not to have no choir.

Sister Pettigrew, president of the Dorcas, said,
"I said I'd never enter this church again if I'd
got to sit all through the service looking at them
disbelieving sinners, excuse me, I mean singers,
for singers are not always professors, and I believe that only professors can sing in a worshipful spirit. I don't want anybody, professors or
not, to sing for me. I don't believe in worship-
ing by proxy. I can't think it's right, and I say
again, I'll never, never enter this church if a
choir comes to disturb the service. As Brother
Grampus says, we don't want a choir, and we are
not going to have one."

"I believe," said Brother Turner, "that singers
are just as good as other folks. Sister Pettigrew is not obliged to look at the choir all the

time. We have good singers in the congregation who are not professors, who sing, I'm sure, in a worshipful spirit. Good music is as essential in a church as good preaching, and I know that music has often done more good than a barrel of sermons.

" The soul may respond to a plaintive chord when it would be untouched by the eloquence of the most noted preacher ; and it is the music, the melody that touches, and not the person or persons who sing. We must have good music, and if we cannot make it ourselves, we must employ those who can. Every soul hungers for music, and this hunger, or the satisfying of it, begets more than we know or think of. A choir is what we want, and I believe we shall have one."

" I've no doubt," exclaimed Sister Snug," thet ther'll be whisperin's an' gigling's, an' onseemly

carryin's on in ther choir, right ahind ther pars-
tor's back, an' afore us all, though they mought
try ter hide an' snicker ahind ther gal'ry curtin.
As Deacon Grampus do very properly say, we're
a-gittin in a despert way ef we're ter look ter sich
pussons fer ter raise up Zion. I've heern tell
o' most scandalyous agoin's on in choirs, an' I
did and do hope I shall never see ther day when
a choir begins its tootin' in our gal'ry. Why,
jest think o' ther quarr'l up ter ther —— church,
all ther choir's doin's."·

"I rise to a point of order," shouted Brother
Tubbs, who had only a far-away love for Sister
Snug. "We did not come here to consider the
short comings or goings on of the choir of the
—— church. Those things don't concern us.
Does Sister Pettigrew and Sister Snug suppose
that we shall scour the earth to find some dis-

reputable people to sing for us. How do they know that our singers, if we have any, will not be professors? There are professors who are singers—there are as many good persons among singers as among other classes of people.

"As to choirs in general, they behave as well as congregations. Members of choirs do not whisper or giggle any more than members of the congregation; they do not go to sleep and snore (he looked hard at Deacon Grampus), and they do not come in late and disturb the service as some members of this congregation do (he looked toward Sister Snug). We intend to secure a choir of ladies and gentlemen, not a minstrel troop, not a Punch and Judy show. The sooner we have a choir, the sooner will we be a live church among live churches."

"I think," said Brother Boom, who was always

exactly balanced between the yea and the nay of any question, and never dared to put down for good his vote or his influence till he knew where the majority was, " I think that the question is whether a choir will help the church or hinder it in its work. If it will aid, let's have the choir; if not, let's not have it."

Both parties applauded this comprehensive speech. Not every man can win the plaudits of opposing factions, and only neutrals (nowheres and nobodies) attempt it.

The next speaker was the sexton. Sextons, generally, if their own emphatic declarations may be accepted, are burdened with many cares and led into early decrepitude in consequence. Of course our sexton was opposed to any addition to his many duties and occupations, and, believing

The Sexton Speaks.

that the no-choir party would prove to be the stronger, hastened to make record.

"I can't think o' enything so onnecessary as er choir. Our ansisters didn't hev no choir, an' didn't they do their duty, an' ain't we proud of 'em? An' who's er goin' ter wait on this choir if we're onlucky 'nough ter git one? Won't they want er warmin' o' ther church ev'ry Sat'dy evenin', fer no choir I ever heard of can sing 'less they learn it jest before han', an' they'll hev ter come an' tune — an' tune.

"See ther expense! We can't efford it, an' ther wood-pile an' ther coal-bin er gittin' lower an' lower. Fires er roarin' all day Sunday, agin ev'ry Wednesday, sometimes of a Friday, an' then ev'ry Sat'dy fer a choir ter ketch ther tune. I tell ye, it's too much, altogether too much.

"An' who'll keep an eye ter ther orgin blower,

the which falls 'sleep reg'ler? As we air now it don't signify whuther er no ther orgin's er goin' er not, 'cause Deacon Grampus' er better leader'n eny orgin, but er choir can't sing 'thout they're helped, an' hev a powerful sight o' waitin' on, an' somebody'll hev ter 'tend ter ther blower—ter begin shakin' him erbout a half er hour afore ther close of ther service ter git him 'roused in time fer ther last tune.

" What with er tendin' fires, an' er fillin' an' er trimmin' lamps, with sweepin's, an' siftin's, an' dustin's, an' er seatin' of ther people, an' er gittin' water fer them thet's allus dry ther busiest time—when ther service is erbout ter begin—an' er passin' ther contribution box, an' er raisin' an' er lowerin' ther winders ter please 'em all, an' er ringin' ther bell, an' er shovellin' paths in ther winter, an' er sprinklin' ashes ter keep ther slipp'ry from fallin', an 'er preparin' ther church fer weddin's an' funerals, an' er carryin' messages, an' er huntin' up lost hymn books, umbrills, parasols, rubbers, gloves, an' other wearin' apparel an' er blowin' ther orgin when the blower can't be woke up, an' er doin arran's too numerous ter mention, an' er bein' in er dozen places ter onct, an' er bein ter blame fer everything except the weather an' er poor sermon, an' per'aps fer thet if the church is too warm or too cold—with all thet ter do—thet's only a fraction of ther whole—the sexton don't hev eny time ter wrastle with the blower, or ter wait on eny choir. Thar's many things we want 'nough sight mor'n a choir, an' one of 'em is an ersistant sexton."

Deacon Gripp, who had had a controversy with the sexton in regard to a north-window, said in substance that sextons were a drug in the market, and that anybody in search of one could take his choice of a dozen any day, and that if the present incumbent— But he was called to order, and took his seat reluctantly.

The discussion went on till all had sung their lay in the major or minor key, and the vote came in favor of the choir, to the surprise, if not the wrath of the no-choir party. A committee of eleven, Deacon Grampus, chairman, was appointed to dictate and to rule in all matters musical.

The sexton was surprised. If he had looked before he leaped, like Brother Boom, he would not be in his present predicament. He changed his mind quickly, however, on receipt of information more favorable to choirs in general, and to make amends wrote a book, "the which this is" in favor of Our Choir. Owing to the forethought and politeness of Deacon Gripp, who took notes at the time, the sexton's assistant is enabled to insert his (the sexton's) speech, and thus make complete the record of the meeting.

III.

THE PITCH.

WHEN the singers in town heard of the committee of eleven, they laughed derisively and said every one: " They need'nt ask me to sing in that choir — to be at the mercy of that committee—a committee of eleven. Oh! O-h!"

But they were in error. A committee of eleven would exist only in name. The official committee would consist of one member, Deacon Grampus. It is true the others, even the whole congregation, might make remarks, and put their fingers in the pie, not to point out the plums, but to show where plums ought to be.

It was a wild desire of Deacon Grampus that singers be invited to meet the committee in the vestry, congregation admitted if desired, and it would certainly desire it, to try their voices and allow the committee to select. But this was curbed, for no self-respecting singer would be a party to such an exhibition. A quartette choir, on its general and floating reputation, was selected, willing to serve for a modest consideration, and came together for rehearsal.

Deacon Grampus was present and spoke from 7.30 to 9.40 by the clock. He was shocked and prostrated by the unexpected result of the meeting, but he was politic enough to take a calm, hopeful, and official view of the situation:

"Ladies an' gentlemen of ther choir: It gives me gret pleasure ter meet ye on this mem'ble 'casion. Ye're ther fust choir we've hed, an' its jest possible ye may be ther last, fer ye're not exactly welcome ter ther hull church, some o' our people's so sot agin a choir. But it'll depend on how ye sing, an' I must tell ye, we're a-lookin' fer something a leetle better'n common. Ye must remember thet a good many good singers 'll be a listenin' ter ye. Thet's why we put off hevin' a choir so long, but ye see, some o' ther congregation kinder thought we orter hev a leetle new timber (Timbre?) Per'aps it's a good idee, time 'll tell.

"Now, I'll tell ye what we want. We want straight-forred music, an' no quaverin's, no holer-

" Now, I'll tell ye what we want."

in's or screamin's — only straight-forred music. We want ther ol' stannards an' plenty ov 'em. Ye'll be watched purty clus. Thar's Brother Biggle. He's a fine bayso-profound, an' wants strong, low pitched notes. An' thar's Sister Sampson with a wonderful nice ear. I don't suppose ye kin git a hair's wedth outer ther way 'thout her knowin' of it. She sets purty well back, an' if ye see her lookin' at ye sharp like, ye may know somethin's wrong. She's a powerful supranny singer, an 'll help ye erlong on ther high notes.

"An' thar's Sister Huxley, a superfine second-singer, an' most pertc'lar on time an' giner'l expression. I suppose she can't be beat—ben a . teacher. She sets in a wing pew, an 'll lift powerful when her pipes are clear an' she knows the tune."

And thus he roamed among the congregation of singers and mentioned nearly every one. Strange that a congregation so endowed with musical ears and voices should yield to foreign talent—that a quartette choir could not be made up among them, but knowing what Deacon Grampus's standard was, the absence of singers may be accounted for.

The deacon's lay had so many lines, and so many *da capo* places in it, that no time remained for rehearsal, and the tenor, the director, said that as only straight-forward music was wanted, they could sing that without rehearsal. " But," he added, " see if they are not dissatisfied."

IV.

THE CHOIR.

"Straight forward music"

N Sunday the choir was in its place. Just before the service began, Deacon Grampus walked into the choir gallery. " I thought," he said graciously, " I'd come up an' give ye a lift in this fust service — jest ter help ye erlong."

Every member of the choir knew the deacon's voice, and his power to exercise it, and his announcement filled them with dismay. The soprano and the alto sank down in the choir-chairs

"I thought I'd come up an' give ye a lift".

as if overcome with sudden faintness, the bass looked, well he looked for his coat and hat, and the tenor gasped and stared. While this dumb play was enacted, Mrs. Grampus, who was, as her husband said, "a very clever woman," saw and understood. She hurried into the gallery:

"Why, John, you are not going to sing, are you? Everybody knows you can sing, and of course the choir can sing if you help them. But what we want to know is if the choir can sing all 'lone, without anybody to help them. Come down. You are not the choir. We don't want to hear you sing to-day."

"Wal, wal, Mirandy, mebby ye're right, but," he continued, turning to the choir, "ef I see ye a-waverin', I shell jine in powerful."

Of course, all were expected to join in, but the choir thought that Deacon Grampus would be near enough where he was, as he sat in a front pew. The service of song was carried out smoothly, but it was evident that the congregation was disappointed. The church was crowded. The town knew all the circumstances preceding and attending the choice of a choir, and as the singers, except the tenor, were well known and recognized as good as any in the place, many came to hear, expecting on this first Sunday something unusual, perhaps something "lively."

But when the choir sang only the old pennyroyal tunes, given out by the pastor, suggested by Deacon Grampus, one of which was "Windham," good old "Windham" in the minor and funereal key, astonishment found expression in words emphatic, and not altogether complimentary to the singers. The people freed their minds as they passed out at the conclusion of the service.

"What a choir!" exclaimed a visitor. "I heard that they were wonderful singers—been practising from the cradle—and that's the best they can do, the first Sunday! The idea of hiring a choir to sing those old grinders!"

"It's almost insulting," said a member of the congregation who wanted something lively, "to give us such hum-drum as that, first time, too, when we expected something new."

"Perhaps they think," growled young Mr. Blister, who was accepted as authority on all kinds of music except his own singing, "that we can appreciate nothing better than 'Windham.' But the organist—he's got some snap."

"If I was the committee," said another lively member, "I'd give that choir to understand quick, or no pay, that we did not hire it—yes, it —it's a good name for it—to sing what we can sing ourselves. But, perhaps Deacon Grampus has been giving them orders. The organist!— wasn't his playing grand! Did you notice the soprano's bonnet?"

"I'm happily disappointed," said a member of the no-choir party. "I was afraid we'd have a concert with jigs and trills, but nothing of the kind. And they sing finely and apparently sincerely. A choir is not so bad after all! I guess we can abide 'em."

But the greater part of the congregation, even the most ardent supporter of the choir, was disappointed. Of course.

As the singers came out of the gallery, Deacon Grampus addressed them:

"Ye did fine, an' no mistake. I ain't heered old 'Windham' so well sung for ten year, but I think, Mr. Bayso-Profound, ye didn't let out quite

(37)

'nough on them low notes, so I jined in powerful (the choir knew it and held its breath for a moment). Ye've started out right. Thet's jest what we want ev'ry Sunday—jest straight-forred music. 'S long's ye give us thet, we're with ye, heart, soul an' voices."

"Old Windham!" ejaculated Mr. Wilkins, the tenor and director, to himself, as he left the church, "if we don't give them something besides 'Windham,' something besides straight-forward music of the Grampus-kind, then there's no life in the choir."

V.

AN INTERLUDE.

"He danced them out."

AS the organ playing had been indifferent and nowhere in particular for a long time — in charge of a teacher who exercised his pupils, and, incidentally the mind of the congregation, a new organist was on duty, and played for the new choir.

He had been given no instructions in regard to straight-forward music. At the close of the service he "danced the congregation out" to the tune of a medley in which there was a strain from "Pinafore," a phrase from the "Beggar's Opera," a group of chords from "Tripping Through the Meadow," a brace from "Rory O'More," and a few bars from "Within a Mile of Edinboro' Town," and major and minor distractions in profusion.

"I'll let 'em know," muttered the organist, as he put on more steam and awoke the great organ as it had not been since it went on duty, "I'll let 'em know that we are here for business."

Only a few members threw notes of protest at the organist, and they changed the key when they found the majority against them. The general verdict on the organ playing was that it was "grand." It was new—had some life in it —something that made the blood run quicker.

The organ had not been aroused before for years, and had been apparently too feeble to clear its throat, but now it was up and doing with a roar.

Already the congregation was dissatisfied with the choir because it had not done what it had been forbidden to do—because it had indulged in no "quaverings," and no "hollerings," and because it had sung straight-forward music, while it praised the organist, and said he was "great," and he was doing exactly what the choir had been ordered not to do.

Now, it is a well-known and admitted fact that no self-respecting choir in this broad land, no choir of ambition and spirit will confine itself to straight-forward music as defined by Deacon Grampus. All honor to them. What are singers-choirs for? To play with a few old tunes, good as they may be, because a fraction of the people have discovered nothing different? Do people dine on mince-pie three times a day because it is good? Is not a change of musical diet as necessary as any?

And there is not a progressive, independent choir to be found that will not attempt to sing, aye, and sing, too, the most difficult composition the world has seen. Again, is the choir, anywhere, crowned with honor. That is the object of "ye trained men and women singers"—to tip to the public in general what it knows not of except by ear, or word of mouth. While only few, comparatively, unlimber tongue in song, yet all, with no exceptions worth mentioning, turn attentive, delighted ear to the melodious phrasing of "music's golden tongue."

And of choirs, it must be said as of folks, that they have their peculiarities. The psychological outline of an average mortal is that of the average choir-subject to varying moods and tenses, and living like the rest of mankind upon a sliding scale, with many accidentals in it of word and temper, relapses into the natural key, not unlike the plank with nails in it used by the Sons of —— as a coasting-place for candidates.

Solos are sweetmeats and solace in the struggle for renown in music—to the singers—not all the hearers heard from. In a well ordered choir the solo-plums must be evenly divided, else the soprano with one looks askance at the alto with two, and with surprise at the director of the choir, who evidently cannot count, or who has a strange, perverted taste; and the bass with one to the tenor's two tells the organ-blower in confidence that deep feeling and a genuine soul-stir are produced solely by low tones. Ah!

there is great fame in solos, and the members of
a choir, presumably all on stilts of the same
height, should have equal shares.

VI.

SOLOS.

—

A S Mr. Wilkins walked homeward, he busied his mind with a solo-programme, and soliloquized thus :—

"Now, let me see. Next Sunday the bass shall spring a solo on them. His notes are low, and he is'nt likely to do any high-galloping for he can't get up there. 'Twouldn't do, of course, to let the soprano sing the first solo,

A tenor Solo.

although by courtesy the ladies should lead. No, the bass must begin, and break the ice, prepare the way for the soprano.

" Then the soprano. Trouble will come, of course, and plenty of it, for if the soprano can't have a chance to take her highest note, and put in a warble on both sides of it, she won't put any heart into her singing. She's right! What's the use of high notes, anyway, if they are not to be tossed out ? They shall not be smothered, if I've anything to say about it.

"Well, then comes the alto leading in song. Her low notes will be like oil on the troubled waters, and will repair the damage done to the peace of mind of the congregation, and the reputation of the choir by the soprano. And — and then look out, for the tenor will sing, and if I don't hang a few notes on the topmost pinnacle of the church-spire, I'm no singer, no tenor worthy the name."

The next Sunday, the service opened with a four-part song, with a few bars of solo-work for each singer. Then the bass came to the front with his solo. It was a surprise, but after Mr. Wilkins had counted up the wry faces — faces distorted by inward anguish — he believed that the majority of the members of the congregation were in sympathy with the choir. At the close of the service, Deacon Grampus exclaimed:

" Wal, ye did purty well on thet fust tune when ye was all a-singin', but why did'nt ye all sing all ther time? Thet's what ye're hired fer. But thet bayso-profound — I dunno — I dunno 'bout him."

The programme arranged by Mr. Wilkins was carried out in every detail. When the soprano toyed with her high note — her vocal pet — and tossed it back and forth like a shuttle-cock, reluctant to let it go, there was here and there in the congregation quiet lamentation, apparently, and evidences of woe. Some were shocked, while others, the majority, exclaimed exultantly, " Well, now, we have a singer worth having ! The other choirs can't crow over us now ! Our choir's good's the best ! "

When the alto's soft tones beat upon those critical tympanums, there was nothing to criticise or censure except the fact that it was a solo. As expected, it healed, in a degree, the wounds inflicted by the soprano, smoothed out some cantankerous wrinkles in mind and forehead, but my pen falters and shakes to record what followed.

When the tenor sent his voice up to the spire's weather-vane, where it perched a moment to rest,

Effect of Tenor's First Solo.

and then soared up into the clouds, then had the climax come. What! Had our church become an opera house—a place of exercise—a gymnasium for screeching mortals and offensive shouters—for so-called singers who disported on any stage like the man in the not-to-be-mentioned play, who sang:

> " O, I'm er ten-or hi-e-i-high;
> I sing ev'ry quaver-qua-hay-ver—
> To-er s'prano's aid I fly-yi-yi,
> If she, as oft, doth wa-hay-ver;
> On me-e-le-e-eens ther al-to,
> Bu-ut nev-er, NEVER tha-hanks me;
> Also, ther (bah!) ha-scratch-y-bas-so—
> A wob-bler-er on high-yi-C-e."

But the choir party clapped its hands in silent glee. The tenor had no fame in the place, being unknown, but fame was laid at his feet now, and many laurels crowned his brow. The town was present, and admitted that no tenor in the neighborhood was his peer.

After the first round of solos had its run, others followed. Mr. Wilkins consulted not the committee of eleven, not because he was guided by a lofty spirit of independence, but because consultation resulted in no solution of the problem. Deacon Grampus was deep in the dumps, and often gave rein to violent tongue when the choir was mentioned. No more did he "join in powerful," but, in evident distress of mind, endured in silence. Sisters Pettigrew and Snug, on the undoubted authority of an observant rear-sitter, and peeker, put cotton in their ears, and leaned their heads, like martyrs on the block, upon the rail of the pew in front that they might not see or hear, and take no part in the "frightful performance."

The wife of a visiting pastor added her fagot to the flame of criticism and revolt by saying, "What a slipshod singer she is! She sang that hymn a half a tone too low all through." What wonderful musical knowledge and sense was here shadowed forth! What a masterly musical performance to sing with the organ, and at the same time to sing a half tone lower than the organ! And if she had sung without accompaniment, and sang a half, or a whole tone too low, how did it mar the melody? A member of the choir party remarked, "We asked the husband to preach, not the wife to meddle with the choir."

But the church grew, and mounted up in popular esteem, and in good works. Vigor and enthusiasm were helpmeets. The congregation in less than a year had nearly doubled, and the

Sunday-school had more than doubled. The no-choir party merely remarked, " Of course, the church was like a man sick with the fever—very low, but there was a turning-point in favor. It came naturally." But they repulsed the idea that medicine had helped the sick man, or that the choir had quickened the pulse of the church.

The choir, however, went its musical way, and it was musical, to the increasing admiration of the choir party, and of the town, and, of course, to the accumulating indignation and scorn of the no-choir party. The year was near its end, and it·was evident that a storm was brewing— a no-choir party storm — which would, doubtless, break forth like a hurricane at the annual meeting not far away.

VII.

SOLO FUGUES.

Discord.

IN the meantime, however, the choir was not in harmony—not on speaking terms with itself. The cause of this discord is not at hand, but it is supposed to have sprung from attempts to solve the solo-problem to the satisfaction of all concerned.

The bass declared, in strict confidence to all his friends, that he had heard sopranos and sopranos, and tenors and tenors, but — Zounds! in all his travels he had not met a soprano or a tenor quite as poor as ours — with so many ragged-edged tones, and no style at all. As for the alto, she could never be much of a singer, anyway. And they were all so disagreeable, too! But, thank heaven, the end was near, and he would soon escape from the din!

And the alto said that all the singers, except the bass, the tenor, and the soprano, were as good as they need be, but that the remainder couldn't do much in such discord and confusion. And the tenor, especially, was so important and over-

bearing, paying attention to the soprano, too —
that she'd never, never sing with him or any of
them again. Just never!

The soprano was indignant. "To think," she
exclaimed, *sub rosa*, to all her friends, "that after
all my study and practice, I've come to this —
singing with such a tenor — such an alto! And
the bass! What a voice! Just drives me wild to
hear it! And what do you think," she continued
in a whisper, "he, the bass, has had the effront-
ery to—to—attempt to—to pay some attention
to me! The idea! Was there ever anything
so insolently audacious? H'm! What a relief
to be free from them! Not another hour would
I sing with them."

But the tenor felt the worst. "Here I've been
practising in Italian atmosphere, imported for
the purpose, getting my voice down to liquid

(56)

flow and smoothness, and up, too, as high as any
of 'em, and now it's dulled and nicked by com-
ing in contact with such husky-wusky, untrained
voices that sing hit or miss all over the page—
anywhere except where they ought to. Humph!
I can't be a whole choir, and do all the singing.

"The bass! Who flattered him into the belief
that he can sing? And the soprano! No wonder the congregation puts cotton in its ears!
But that alto—language fails. She had the
audacity to suggest how I should make the solo-
appointments. A very disagreeable and presum-
ing woman! If I ever sing within a mile of that
alto again, with that bass, or that soprano—with
such a jarring, discordant company, it will be for
the same reason that men go to jail—for pun-
ishment."

But the tenor, the soprano, the alto, and the

bass agreed on one point. While it was possible — barely possible — that the organist might
teach beginners the rudiments (more likely snarl
up their fingering) on a seraphine, and be useful
and ornamental in various occupations, yet there
was one thing he could not in reason expect to
do, and that was, to play a church organ.

" Why," exclaimed the director of the choir,
" when we want to show the richness and
smoothness of our voices—the purity of tone—
he'll draw the stops to all the noisy pipes,
and stamp out a jig on the pedals — just smother
us in a blast of trumpets; and when we want
help—want a sympathetic chord to lift us over
a high or ragged place, he plays low—limps along
pianissimo a good half behind. He appears to
be afraid of the organ till the congregation is
dismissed, and then—and then he throws himself

at it, wrestles with it to a painful-to-see degree, till it's a wonder there's any organ left. Why, that organ won't last a year if he continues to play, and the choir—well, the choir's worn out now."

And the organist said: "If I play another year, I hope they'll get some singers—somebody that can keep within a rod of the key. Why, I've had to open all the stops, couple on the big organ, and nearly blow the whole fabric to pieces to bring them back on to the key! What are such folks trying to sing for, anyway? Shades of Mozart! What would they have done without me!"

VIII.

A MEDLEY.

T HE meeting in the interest of harmony and music had its run, and its members allowed their tongues to run beyond the limit of reason and politeness. A rumor ran, too, to the effect that the no-choir party had a majority, and would rule with a rod of iron — ruling out instanter the choir to a quick-step movement. The no-choir party took the floor immediately, and set at liberty to run rampant, broadside after broadside of criticism into the camp of the enemy — the choir party. At last Mr. Wilkins could keep his seat no longer, and he sprang into the breach between talkers. He was a man of affairs as well as a good singer. He was wise and diplomatic.

"Ladies and gentlemen: I have no right to speak here, but the accused should not be condemned until heard. This meeting, or what has been said, is a great surprise to me. You cannot mean what you say — you, the good men and women of this church and town — you cannot, in your sober moments, think so ill of the choir.

"There is a reporter present, and he will have all in the paper to-morrow in bold type, and will you, Deacon Grampus, pillar in the church and town, read with pleasure that you said at this meeting that the choir in your church is a 'set of hollering nuisances'? You did not mean to say that respectable men and women, doing their duty as well as they know it, are nuisances. No, you did not intend to say anything so impolite. When we began, you wanted plain music. We gave you plain music, and you were dissatisfied. Of course. You hired us to do what other choirs do. And we have sung as others sing, exerting ourselves, and doing the utmost possible to please you.

"We could do no more if we were paid five thousand dollars a year each. We have rendered the best service we are capable of, and no man can do more, and our reward, even if some of you are not pleased, ought to be something better than spiteful criticism and hard names. We do not deserve this treatment at your hands —it is unworthy of you. Now," continued Mr.

Wilkins, in the smoothest tenor voice, "if you consider it independent of any other question, if you look at it dispassionately, wasn't it pretty good singing after all?"

The tenor was known as a fiery man, all tenors are fiery, but this mild yet plain spoken address blunted the edge of criticism, really disarmed the opposition, and paved the way for what was to come. The silence that fell at the conclusion of Mr. Wilkins' remarks was painful and unbroken for a half a minute, except by Deacon Grampus, who tip-toed around to the reporter, probably to keep an eye on him, and perhaps to collar him if he attempted to escape before his copy was properly expunged.

At last Brother Splinter arose, and the audience braced itself for the storm to come. Brother Splinter was a quiet man, chary of words except in emergencies — and then he could supply a whole village. He would speak the truth and send it home, like a wad in a gun-barrel. He had influence, too, a big pile of it, in the bank, growing bigger every day.

"Ladies and gentlemen: I attended a worldly meeting the other day, not so worldly as this, if I may judge by the temper and tenor (not Mr. Wilkins) of this, in which a man arose and criticised some statement of the speaker. The speaker replied: 'I wasn't addressing you in particular, but the audience as a whole. If you don't like what I say, the proper course for you is to take your departure,— there's room enough out of doors,—or hold your peace. You have no right to disturb this meeting because you are not in sympathy with it.'

"Now," continued Mr. Splinter, who had

worked his way from the rear of the vestry to the platform, "if this choir is so intolerable to some members of the congregation, how can they endure and remain.   Is it not extraordinary that these members have endured this torture, have put themselves on the rack, and although suffering terribly, got onto the rack as often as they could and stayed on as long as possible?   Why! brothers and sisters, there are people not a mile away who are never happy till they are up to their ears in hot water, and when they are well in, they splash around, enjoy themselves, and try to scald others, instead of quietly slipping out and going their way, when the majority is against them — when facts, reason, sense stare them in the face in determined opposition.

"Sometimes minorities are right, and then all honor to them for contending for the right, but such is not the case here. What is the minority here? Its members, strictly speaking, may be counted twice on the fingers of both hands, and why are these members opposed to a choir? I'll tell you," said Mr. Splinter, raising his voice an octave at one jump, "they are opposed because they made up their minds in advance — long before the choir came — to oppose, to hinder, to belittle the choir in every way possible to the bitter end.

"Some of the early objectors have been won over in spite of themselves, but the few, the paltry half dozen, adhere like a porous plaster to the compact they made with themselves, before they saw or heard the choir, never to yield, too proud to give in, but obstinate enough to hold out. And not one of this little minority has any definite knowledge of music, and the opinions of any one on music wouldn't be quoted at a herring's value in the market. (Mr. Splinter was a dealer in fish.)

"And is not this wee bit of a minority just full and running over with selfishness? They ask us—this church and congregation—to yield to them—to give up the pleasures of music—to go back to the humdrum doodle-doo to please them—to please them, fighting in spite for a whim and not for any principle, and not for the good of the church. We will not yield to them! We ought to rise in christian wrath and indignation and stamp out this spirit of evil—it is nothing else—that has menaced our peace and made us a laughing-stock.

"The affairs of churches, even, must, in a measure, be conducted on business principles. If there be elements of discord, we must proceed in a business, as well as a christian way, to bring them into harmony or cast them out. If the minority can't abide us, let its members get their baggage ready and go by the next train, or for-ever hold their peace. Let us rise and say, and mean it, that we will not longer submit to the offensive domination of a flaw-picking minority.

"This meeting, instead of being an indignation meeting to throw stones and harder words at the choir, ought to be a ratification-congratulatory meeting—a meeting to thank the choir for the good service rendered this church. It's a good choir, as good as any church in this town has or ever had—not only good as a choir, but also good as to the standing of its members in the com-munity. The fact that our choir is composed of ladies and gentlemen, in the full meaning of the terms, who have done their duty conscientiously, ought to have saved them and the church this humiliation, even if their singing had been unsatisfactory to every one of us.

"The congregation and Sunday-school have been largely increased during the year. Once more is there life in the old church we love so well. Did the choir have any part in this renewal of vigor? If not, who or what added new life? And what did this little minority do toward this good result? Why, its members seemed to have no more important business during the year than to whisper in corners, and to point their fingers at the choir; and, shameful to relate, put cotton in their ears, and, worse yet, made a parade of the fact.

"The choir deserves our gratitude, and any amends we can make for its unhandsome treatment at the hands of the minority, and, therefore, I move that this meeting do humbly apologize to the choir—take back what has been said to-night, and give instead a vote of thanks—all in one motion I put it."

This was carried with enthusiasm. The meeting, or some of its members, had been aroused to a normal sense in thought and action, and a solid yea vote was the result.

"And now," said Brother Splinter, "there is another way to reward the choir. We are going to have a choir the next year, and we cannot get a better choir than the one we've had. Therefore, I move that the choir, if it will serve, and the organist, also, be engaged for another year, and, to save time, I embody in the same motion this, that the pastor, the superintendent of the Sunday-school, and the leader of the choir be the committee—the only committee—on music, subject to no one, nothing, except the good taste and sense of its members."

A dozen voices seconded the motion, and it was carried without a dissenting vote, and it is believed that all voted. The choir was present, and sang, by request, "Should auld acquaintance be forgot," and sang it so softly, feelingly, that it was indeed a benediction, and many, including Deacon Grampus and Sister Snug, were notably "teary around the lashes."

After the choir had entered upon the work of another year, Sister Pettigrew remarked: "Well, the choir's improving. I begin to like the singing," and Sister Snug said softly, apparently much subdued in spirit, "It don't sound so bad after one gits 'customed to 't," and Deacon Grampus admitted that "the church might go further an' fare wuss," and that "thar's no denyin' ther fac, they do give them ol' tunes a remark'ble fine settin'."

Auld Lang Syne.

IX.

EPITHALAMIUM.

Harmony.

NUPTIAL song should follow here to commemorate the triple union — the choir with the church, and the members of the choir with each other.

True love never runs smoothly till the goal be reached, where and when the way widens, and delightful vistas "spring to view" on every hand.

The members of the choir, determined on separation with not less than a mile between them, consented to blend voices another year. When Winter was packing up and moving out, and Spring was laying carpets, beautifully shaded green, preparatory to moving in, the tenor and the alto were married (soprano and bass, best man and woman), and not long thereafter, when the new tenant, Spring, had hung her tasseled curtains up and placed flowers in the windows, the "bans" of the soprano and the bass were announced.

And the organist, soliloquizing on these matrimonial complications, as he drew out all the couplers and stops and walked around on the pedals, and threw a wholesale snatching of chords from "Mendelssohn's Wedding March," and a few connecting links from "The Spring Fairy" into an exit-quick-as-you-can postlude, muttered to himself, soft and low: "Just what I expected when they wouldn't speak to each other last year! Humph! An organist don't have time to do any courting; if he did, it's just possible that tenor wouldn't be wearing so many smiles these days."

The only person not contented and satisfied with life and its surroundings at this good time was the organ-blower. He relieved his mind, crowded to bursting, with thoughts more or less dangerous to the welfare of the tenor and the bass.

"I did hope," said the organ-blower savagely, "that the bass and the tenor would have to go.

There's a 'spiracy between 'em. I know it. I never fell 'sleep once — not once — but this 's a free country, and I guess I can close my eyes and nod my head if I want to, without asking leave of the tenor or the bass.

"For some time, I felt pricks in my legs I couldn't account for — in the summer thought 'twas skeeters—but at last I see the bass drawin' away the black-board pointer with a pin in the end of it, and again, I caught the tenor doin' the same thing. Now I know why I'm covered all over with jabs and scratches, and stuck full of pinholes. If I thought the organist was in the 'spiracy (I see him laughin' behind a book) I'd stop his wind when he's tryin' to show off in perludin' or antiludin'. But that bass and that tenor—how 'm I goin' to get even with them?"

But after the choir, came other improvements, and among them a mechanical blower that required no shaking or black-board pointer reminding—a blower subject and immediately obedient to the organist.

And the choir continues to sing, and to lead in song—to lead the congregation up to the highest appreciation and enjoyment of music — the old, the new, even the lively — aye, and up to the yielding to its "soft persuasive voice" that "sweetly soothes and never betrays."

And the congregation — in harmony sings in harmony — sings as it never sang before, for —

"The soul of music slumbers in the shell,
Till waked and kindled by the master's spell;
And feeling hearts, touch them but lightly, pour
A thousand melodies unheard before."

X.

POSTLUDE.

"Saw me taking notes."

IT has been noised abroad, probably through the agency of the spying organ-blower, who saw me taking notes behind a pillar (not Deacon Grampus), that I am writing a book about the choir. Deacon Gripp, who sits in the wall-aisle, next pew-door to the hottest furnace-pipe, and who imagines that he is in sole command (great mistake) of the north window, which abuts on

(78)

his church property, and who opens this window every winter Sunday, to the great annoyance of adjacent pew-holders, especially a near sitter with a bald head (a good man), which window I closed last Sunday three times at the request of seventeen, forty-two, and twenty-seven persons respectively—

This man, Deacon Gripp, I say, announces that with the help of Sister Snug, who sits in a back pew near the big door, and who wants to know, every cold Sunday, when the big door is open to admit the congregation, why there's no fire in the church (when it's sizzling hot at the other end), and if it is not about time to look for a "saxton" who can attend to his duties, and give some attention to the comfort of the people—announces, I say, that with the help of Sister Snug and Brother Quick, who wants to be sexton himself, "just long enough to show the people what a sexton ought to do "—

Deacon Gripp announces, I say again, that with the help of these worthies he is compiling a work (calls it a work) entitled "Our Sexton," which he says, pompously, will be given to the press immediately.

I improve this opportunity to show forth that I know just how all their slings and arrows are pointed — dull as crow-bars — Gripp's, Snug's, Quick's, and that I deny their gross exaggerations and allegations, one and all, tee-total, and that I shall not resign so long as strength remains to keep an eye, and to clap a hand, to that north-window as often, on a cold day, as Deacon Gripp, or any other man, durst open it.

THE SEXTON.

XI.

AN ECHO.

A FTER I had wrote this Storey, I gave it toe a noospaper man toe run his Ey threw it. My Granfarthers grate Unkl was vary litrary and so was my Farther and I hav wrote Poartrey all threw my life,

"Not one word of mine.

tho not for Publickton, and olltho I can mak a dubble rime in enny line (see, it kums nacherul) I'm not shure on fine pints of Sin Tacks,

Gramur and Genral Logick. So I wanted ther noospaper man toe see if Ide made no mistak.

When he brot back ther Storey he sed I orter get a Prynter and he volenterred toe tak it rite down toe him. As Ide hed sum talk with a Prynter bout it I told him toe go ahed. Toe my Sub Cequent Sorrew I did not look at ther Storey agen supposin it was as I had wrote it.

I happnd intoe ther Prynters Offiss just as he was a bindin it up intoe a book. What was my Dismay toe see on ther furst page — Orthur Of and Cetterry. Nothink could be farther from my thots. But that was not er Sarcumstence toe what I discuvered as I turnd toe ther Storey.

Not wun wurd of mine could I find frum Over — ther — ther — what's thet — toe ther end not wun. Ther Prynter chuckeled, ther raskill, and I beleev hees an Erkompliss of ther noospaper man. If I could not put in this which I've hedded "Noat of Protess" the Publick Ey shuld nevar look up on it.

THER SEXTON ORTHUR OF OUER QUIRE.

THE ECHO'S ECHO.

And the public eye did not look upon "this which hedded 'Noat of Protess,'" but owing to the " hurry" (the first and the last) of the printer, neither time nor opportunity remained "to run an eye threw" the " noat " itself.

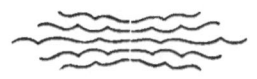